D0612003

THE MUPPETS

Little, Brown and Company

Hachette Book Group
237 Park Avenue, New York, NY 10017
Visit our website at www.lb-kids.com

Little, Brown and Company is a division of Hachette Book Group, Inc.
The Little, Brown name and logo are trademarks of
Hachette Book Group, Inc.

The publisher is not responsible for websites (or their content) that are not
owned by the publisher.

First Edition: October 2011

The characters and events portrayed in this book are fictitious.
Any similarity to real persons, living or dead, is coincidental and
not intended by the author.

ISBN: 978-0-316-18303-1

10   9   8   7   6   5   4   3   2   1

RRD-C

Printed in the United States of America

THE MUPPETS

THE MOVIE JUNIOR NOVEL

Adapted by Katharine Turner
Based on a script by Jason Segel & Nick Stoller

L B

LITTLE, BROWN AND COMPANY
New York   Boston

Walter was having the dream again.

He and his best friend, Gary, were little kids, sitting in front of the TV, watching their favorite show in the whole world—*The Muppet Show*. Walter gave Gary a cheerful grin as they sang along with the theme song.

"It's time to meet the Muppets, on *The Muppet Show* tonight!"

And that was when they spotted Animal heading for the front of the screen. But instead of staying inside the TV, the Muppet drummer pushed right through the glass and into Walter's living room!

"Wait! Animal!" Kermit the Frog wailed from inside the television. "You can't climb out of the TV. Someone get him!"

Before they knew what was happening, Gary and Walter were surrounded by a mass of Muppets chasing Animal around. Even Walter's hero, Kermit, hopped into the living room to join in the chase.

"I'm terribly sorry about this," Kermit apologized. "Hey, Walter, why don't you join us? C'mon, the show's about to start!"

Walter looked nervously at his best friend. Him? Join the Muppets? But Gary nodded with encouragement and even gave him the double thumbs-up. The Muppets began diving back into the TV screen. It was now or never for Walter. Kermit stretched out his hand and, with one deep breath, as the last Muppet vanished back into the television, Walter threw himself in after them.

And then he hit the glass screen with a resounding *clunk*!

Dusting himself off, Walter got to his knees and pressed his hands against the TV screen. He sighed.

He wasn't a Muppet. He would never be a Muppet, and no amount of banging and yelling on the screen was going to help.

Somewhere, in a small bedroom, in a small house, in a small town, an alarm clock rang out. It was another beautiful day in Smalltown, USA, and Gary opened his eyes with a smile. In the bed opposite, his best friend in the whole world, Walter, was already wide awake. Their bedroom walls were covered in posters, newspaper clippings, fan art, and signed photographs, all with one thing in common: the Muppets.

"Morning, Walter," Gary said. He could barely contain his excitement. "Today's the day!" The tall guy wiggled his toes in excitement. He was so tall that his feet stuck out at the end of the bed.

"I know!" Walter bounced out of bed. He was a lot shorter than his best friend, and...well...he was not like other humans. But Gary never pointed that out. "I could hardly sleep."

"Oh, buddy," Gary said with a frown. "Did you have the dream again?"

Walter went over to a big old jar of coins and jingled the pennies, nickels, dimes, and quarters inside. There were just enough coins to creep up over a red line drawn near the top of the jar. "Er...no."

Walter had been saving every penny for years, wishing away the days until he could finally make the trip to Los Angeles to fulfill his dream—to visit the Muppet Studios. He had watched every single episode of *The Muppet Show* over and over, and meeting the Muppets was his only goal in life. Finally, today was the day.

"Muppet Studios! L.A., here we come!" Walter stared dreamily at the jar. In just a few hours he'd be there, meeting his heroes.

"We'd better get a move on," Gary said, hopping out of bed. "Don't want to miss the bus."

The guys headed for the bathroom, passing walls plastered with photos of the two of them together, making their scout salutes, celebrating their joint bar mitzvahs, getting ready for prom, pulling wacky faces in a photo booth.

"Hey, Gary," Walter said, squeezing some toothpaste onto his brush. "Maybe Kermit will be there?"

Gary frowned. He loved the Muppets just as much as Walter did, but he didn't want his buddy to get his hopes too high. "I don't think so, Walter. The Muppets broke up their act, remember? They don't use the studios for anything but tours anymore."

"That's just an Internet rumor." Walter shook his head. "Like there being a country called Turkey."

Gary paused for a moment. "Actually, I think there is a country called Tur—"

"Muppet Studios!" Walter interrupted, too excited to listen.

Gary didn't finish correcting his friend. It didn't matter. Walter and Gary weren't just roommates, they were best buds. BFFs. Nothing would ever come between them. They'd been best friends since they were little kids, and now they were finally living their dream of visiting the Muppet Studios together. Everything was great. Except, well, maybe not quite everything.

He had never admitted it to Gary, but Walter had always felt a little out of place in Smalltown, USA. He wasn't sure if it was his big googly eyes, or his fuzzy hair, or maybe the fact that he was four feet shorter than Gary.... He just knew he didn't quite fit in. But he also knew the answer was out there, somewhere. Walter had always had a crazy feeling that if he could just visit the Muppet Studios and meet his heroes, his whole life would fall into place.

Gary, however, loved everything about Smalltown, USA. And why wouldn't he? Not only did he share a house with his best friend in the whole world, he had the best girl as well. He'd been dating his sweetheart, Mary, for ten whole years, and for ten whole years they'd been planning a romantic vacation to L.A.

Mary was still hard at work teaching her shop class outside the local elementary school when Gary arrived with a crumpled bunch of daffodils in his hand. At first he didn't see her — just a crowd of kids standing near a car. Then the tiny redhead slid out from underneath the car wearing a pristine summer dress and a smile.

"And that's how you fix a carburetor!" Mary announced to a cheering class full of sixth graders. The bell sounded loudly. "And that's spring vacation!"

The class sighed.

"We'll be back in school in two weeks!" she said.

The class cheered again and ran off.

"You look amazing," Gary said, presenting Mary with the slightly crumpled flowers.

"They're sweet." She gave him a big smile and dusted off her dress. "I'm so excited for our vacation!"

Mary pulled a long list from her pocket. At the top it read GARY AND MARY'S THINGS TO DO IN L.A. She had been looking forward to their vacation for the longest time.

"It's going to be so romantic," Mary said with a sigh. "I've always dreamt of seeing Los Angeles."

"I know. Walter can't wait, either," Gary replied, wrapping her up in a big hug. "Are you sure you don't mind him coming with us?"

"Of course," Mary said, a little disappointed. Then she found her smile again and made it extra bright for Gary. "Walter loves the Muppets. Just as long as we get our anniversary dinner."

"You betcha!" Gary beamed. "Walter loves dinners! And anniversaries! And birthdays. And Christmas…"

"I meant just me and you," Mary said loudly. "No Walter."

"Oh, right. Got it! Of course we can! It'll be the most romantic dinner ever," Gary agreed. She was such a great girl. "I'll see you later. L.A., here we come!"

Mary watched Gary leave and couldn't help but feel a little sad. She'd been looking forward to their romantic vacation for years, but how romantic was it going to be with Walter along for the ride? Gary and Walter were inseparable.

It wasn't that she didn't like Walter. He was one of her best friends! She just wished she and Gary could spend a little more time alone together. They'd been dating for ten years, and nothing ever changed. Maybe they'd get a chance to be alone in

L.A., at their anniversary dinner. Mary sat down on the hood of the truck and daydreamed. She imagined herself in Paris, Gary riding toward her on a horse, wearing a white top hat and tails, a sparkly diamond ring in his hand. If only Gary would propose. Then everything would be okay....

Later that afternoon, Mary, Gary, and a very excited Walter gathered at the bus stop in the center of town. They waved to all their friends: the postman, the baker, the policeman. Everyone was happy in Smalltown, USA.

"I can't believe we're finally doing this," Walter gasped as a big, shiny, silver bus pulled to a halt in front of them.

Mary nodded, excited for her romantic vacation. Gary nodded, excited for his trip with his two favorite people in the entire world. And Walter

trembled with excitement, certain he was board-
ing the bus not just to find the Muppets, but also
to find his destiny.

Good-bye, Smalltown, USA, and hello, the rest
of his life.

I can't believe it!" Gary spun around, taking in the wonders of the big city with wide eyes. "Los Angeles!"

"Hello, vacation," Mary said, grinning.

"We're really here!" Walter was almost too excited to stand still. "City of dreams."

Only L.A. didn't look so much like a city of dreams. The gang had jumped off the bus in the center of downtown Hollywood and, well, it was kind of gross. The buildings were grimy, there were fanny pack–toting tourists everywhere, and everything looked like it needed a good scrubbing. They were a long way from Smalltown, but it didn't matter. They were happy to be there. What could possibly go wrong?

The three friends made their way to the Muppet Studios. Looking up at it, Walter couldn't believe his eyes. At last, he had arrived. He'd loved the Muppets all his life, saved every penny for years, traveled all the way across the country by bus, and now here he was, standing in front of the Muppet Studios....

And they were a mess. He tried hard not to show how sad he was, but it was difficult. The buildings were run-down and boarded up, with almost every window broken. There wasn't a trace of Muppet magic to be seen—just a small handwritten sign advertising tours for fifty cents. An elderly Chinese couple stood staring at the sign, looking confused. Walter was just as perplexed.

"What happened?" he whispered.

"Well, it *is* midweek." Gary tried to come up

with a reason for the run-down state of the studios and the lack of tourists. "And it's kinda out of season?"

"But everyone loves the Muppets," Walter replied. *Don't they?*

Before Gary or Mary could come up with a response, an old man in a tour-guide uniform appeared beside them.

"Well, it's a better turnout than yesterday," he muttered to no one in particular. "Always awkward talking to yourself. You here for the tour?"

"Yes, sir," Walter confirmed, starting to feel excited again. Perhaps all the surprises were inside. Perhaps it was just the outside of the studios that looked so bad.

"Then welcome to the original Muppet Studios," the tour guide said. He threw a handful of glitter and ash up into the air, and then coughed as he inhaled it. It was the most glamorous coughing fit Walter had ever witnessed. "Where dreams come true."

Inside the studio lot, Walter closed his eyes, rubbed them hard, and opened them again. Yep, this was really happening. All the things he'd dreamed of seeing were there: the "Pigs in Space" rocket, The Great Gonzo's cannon, even the famous *Muppet Show* sign. Except the sign was missing an all-important *O*, the cannon was covered in dust, and the rocket was broken. That was the last straw—he was officially heartbroken. The dream was over.

"Yeah, so this is where they stored the props." The tour guide nodded toward the room of broken bits and pieces. "And here they are, in all their glory...."

"Excuse me, sir," Walter piped up. There had to be something here worth seeing. "Would it be possible to go into the auditorium itself? The Muppet Theater?"

The guide clucked his tongue and sucked his teeth. "Sorry, sonny. Nope. Condemned since the early nineties. Structurally unsound. Health and Safety just wouldn't allow it."

Gary placed a hand on his buddy's shoulder. It was hard enough for him and Mary to see the place this way—he knew it had to be super hard on Walter.

"Now, this here used to be Kermit's office," the tour guide explained as they passed a small building. "It's perfectly preserved inside, just as Kermit left it. It is by far the highlight of the tour."

Everyone stopped and gasped.

The tour guide nodded, then started walking again. "You really should see it someday."

Everyone sighed.

"Now," he went on, "this next building is where they stored all the rope and medium-gauge wire they used on the show. Exciting, right? Let's go inside and take a look...."

But instead of following the rest of the group inside, Walter hung back just a little. This was it:

his only chance to see inside Kermit's office. *The* Kermit the Frog. His hero! He had to try. Once the rest of the tour group had vanished into the storage shed, Walter opened the door to the building. Inside, everything was just as the tour guide had said it would be, just as Kermit had left it when he had walked away from the Muppet Studios for the last time. A thick layer of dust covered every surface, but otherwise it was just how Walter had imagined it. At last, something was going right on this vacation.

"And this is Kermit's old office," barked a loud voice as the opposite door to the office slammed open.

"Or so we've been *toad*," replied another voice, with a guffaw.

Not knowing what else to do, Walter hid. He didn't want to get in trouble; he'd just wanted to see inside Kermit's office. Peering out from his hiding place, his eyes widened with wonder at the sight in front of him. He knew he'd recognized those voices! They belonged to Muppets! Specifically, to Statler and Waldorf. It was almost too strange for Walter to see them standing just a few feet away and not heckling the cast of *The Muppet Show* from their balcony box. But they weren't alone. Closely following them was a tall businessman in a suit and a cowboy hat, accompanied by several of his associates. He looked around the dusty office and gave Statler and Waldorf a big smile.

"Well, as you know, gentlemen, I've loved the Muppets since I was a boy, and I, Tex Richman, can't think of a better way to honor the Muppets than to make this beautiful studio into a museum." Tex held his arms up and gestured around the office. "A shrine, if you will. I'll call this room 'The Kermit the Frog's Old Office Room.'"

"Well, I guess if they're going to sell the old place, I'm glad it's going to a fan," Statler said, nodding to himself. "I had some of the happiest times of my life here."

"You did?" Waldorf sounded surprised.

"Sure." Statler laughed. "Whenever I got into my car to drive home at night!"

They all seemed pretty happy, but there was something about Tex that made Walter uncomfortable. He just didn't trust the guy. Maybe it was the ten-gallon hat, or the shifty grin, or the fact that he had a terrifying-looking Muppet dragon in his entourage who kept eyeing Walter's hiding place. Walter really hoped no one could hear his knees knocking together.

"Now, here's the standard rich-and-famous contract Kermit signed thirty-five years ago," Waldorf said, producing a huge pile of paper.

"And that contains the deed to this property?" Tex asked, eyeing the contract greedily. "The studios and the theater?"

"Exactly." Waldorf nodded. "Now, this contract

is one hundred percent ironclad, with one minor exception. I should let you know that if the Muppets can raise the ten million dollars it would cost to buy this building before the contract expires, then they will get their studio back. But as it stands, the contract expires"—he paused to take a closer look at the fine print—"in two weeks. At which point the property is yours." Tex nodded. Satisfied their business was complete, Statler and Waldorf left the office mumbling to themselves about plot points and exposition.

Walter missed what they were saying because Tex had turned to his cohorts, looking altogether less friendly. This was getting scary.

"Gentlemen," he whispered, "there's oil under this studio. I can smell it. And more important, the geographical survey I had done says there definitely is. In two weeks we tear this place down and start drilling. Ah, those Muppets, they think they're so funny. Well, it looks like the joke's about to be on them. Maniacal laugh. Maniacal laugh."

Everyone in Tex's gang broke out into evil laughter. Walter stifled a yelp. Tex just kept repeating the words "maniacal laugh," which Walter would have thought was pretty weird if he hadn't been in shock. Sneaking back out the door he had come in, Walter ran as fast as his legs would carry him until he found Gary, Mary, and the rest of the tour group.

"What's up, little buddy?" Gary asked.

"ARRRRRRRRRRRRRRRRRGGGGGH!" Walter screamed. And screamed. And kept screaming.

It kinda went on for a while.

Three

Walter carried on screaming all on the way to the bus. And then he screamed all the way to the hotel. And then he kept screaming all the way to the room. Where he did not stop screaming.

"Well, if he's just going to do this for some time, we could head out and grab a quick bite to eat," Mary suggested, picking up her purse.

Gary shook his head. This was going to take some serious action. Luckily, he was a serious-action man.

"Sorry, buddy," he said as he stretched his arm back and then slapped Walter so hard that the little guy flew across the room. But on the plus side, the screaming stopped.

"We've got to find Kermit!" Walter popped up

from behind the bed and began to run around the room, wailing, "Argh! We've got to save the studio! We've got to find Kermit!"

"Slow down!" Gary tried to calm Walter.

Walter took a deep breath, stopped, and slumped over with his head in his hands. "You don't understand," he moaned, Tex Richman's maniacal laugh echoing in his head. "This is terrible. Just terrible."

Mary and Gary looked at each other. What were they going to do?

"And then, when he was alone, he said" — in the backseat of the gang's rental car, Walter cleared his throat and did his best Tex Richman impression for Gary and Mary — " 'There's oil under this studio, see? I'm gonna tear it to the ground, see? Sweet, sweet oil, see?' "

"People still talk like that?" Mary asked, staring out the car window.

"Maybe that's just how he sounded in my head." Walter shrugged. "Either way, we've got to find Kermit! He'll know just what to do."

For lack of a better plan, the three friends had rented a car and decided to drive around L.A. until they found Kermit. Walter couldn't just sit by and watch Tex Richman destroy the Muppet Studios, but what could he do to stop him? He was just Walter. This was definitely a job for the Muppets.

"Yeah, but how do we find him?" Mary frowned and tied her red hair back in a ponytail. "No one's seen Kermit in years, not since the Muppets broke up."

Walter made a face. He just needed an idea. Just a hint. Just the smallest clue. He stared out the window as they passed a hot dog stand and a man selling maps to the stars' homes.

"Stop the car!" Walter yelped. "I have an idea!"

Two minutes later, Walter, Gary, and Mary were

happily eating some of the tastiest hot dogs in all of the USA.

"These are delicious," Gary mumbled through a mouthful of hot dog. "But how are we going to find Kermit?"

"The hot dog guy said he lives in Bel Air," Mary chimed in. "And that he's become some sort of recluse."

But that wasn't enough to dissuade Walter. At least they had somewhere to start looking. "Let's go to Bel Air," he said, throwing his arms around his friends' shoulders. "We'll find him, I know we will. To Bel Air!"

Their newfound sense of optimistic purpose didn't last long. Hours later, the gang was still driving around in circles, no closer to finding Kermit or saving the Muppet Studios. Gary moaned and said, "We're never going to find him!"

The sun had set, and Walter was crestfallen, his shoulders slumped.

"We've been driving for hours," Gary said. "Call it a day?"

"Uh, guys?" Mary tapped Gary on the shoulder.

"We can't give up!" Walter wailed.

"Really, guys?" Mary moved on to tapping Walter, but neither of the guys was paying any attention to her.

"Even if we end up searching for days! Weeks!" Walter yelled.

"GUYS!"

"What?"

Mary leaned across the front seat and pointed out the window. Right in front of them was a huge mansion with grand, ornate gates. Gates decorated with Kermit's face.

"Maybe he lives there?" she asked.

Kermit's mansion was amazing. It was a huge, sprawling estate surrounded by gravel driveways, manicured lawns, and one great big electric fence.

"How are we going to get to Kermit?" Gary

stared at the wall in front of them. There wasn't a single spot where they could possibly sneak in.

Walter pulled himself up to his full height. "Throw me over the wall," he said with steely determination.

"Are you sure?" Gary asked as his brave buddy hopped into his open arms.

"Throw me," Walter repeated, his eyes on the prize. "Over the wall."

Folding his floppy friend into a ball, Gary was preparing for the throw when a voice interrupted them.

"Um, excuse me?"

The three of them turned to see a small figure silhouetted by a bright white light. A heavenly chorus sounded in their ears as their eyes adjusted to the light and they realized that it wasn't a small person. It was a larger-than-average-size frog. It was Kermit. Which was way easier to work out once the bus driving the choir, singing way too loud for a residential neighborhood, had passed by and continued down the road.

"Hi, ho," Kermit said. "Can I help you?"

Being addressed by his own personal hero was just too much for Walter. He took one look at the frog and passed out in Gary's arms.

A few minutes later, Walter opened his eyes to find himself inside...but where? The house was like a time warp. It looked like a fantasy pad from the early 1980s—shag carpets, sunken sofas, a rock-lined fireplace.... It also looked like it hadn't been cleaned since the '80s.

"I think he's coming to," Walter heard Gary say.

"Where am I?" Walter whispered. Surely, they couldn't be...

"It's okay, Walter," Gary reassured his buddy. "We're in Kermit's house."

Walter sat straight up. "This...this is Kermit's house?"

"Well, not really," Kermit said, shrugging. "I just stop by once a week to pick up the mail and clean out the pool filters."

"Then where do you live?" Gary asked. They were all kind of relieved that Kermit wasn't holed up alone in this place. Obviously, he must be living in some super-cool pad in the Hollywood Hills.

"Over in the park," Kermit said. "There's a pond in the abandoned zoo with some nice lily pads."

"You live in a pond?" Mary asked. Well, it was one kind of pad.

"Sure," Kermit confirmed. "It's kind of peaceful, actually."

Gary and Mary looked to Walter to reply. But it's difficult to speak when you're staring at your idol with your mouth hanging open. So Gary started for him.

"Kermit," he said. "My friend Walter heard some disturbing news today."

"Oh, yeah?" Kermit looked concerned. "What's that, Walter?"

Walter upgraded from starstruck to terrified. "Tex Richman...oil baron..." he stuttered.

"Yes!" Kermit listened to Walter and nodded. "Oil baron Tex Richman the philanthropist is going to buy our old theater and turn it into a Muppet museum. Isn't that great?"

"No, oil!" Walter yelled before losing his voice again.

"What Walter is trying to say," Mary translated, "is that Tex Richman has a secret plan to tear down the theater and drill for oil."

"What?" Kermit looked shocked. "That's terrible!"

"And the only way to save it is to raise ten million dollars," Gary explained.

"Ten million dollars?" Kermit repeated. "But

that's impossible. The only way to raise that kind of money would be to put on a show. And we haven't done that in a long time...."

Kermit took a moment for himself as he walked down memory lane in his head. "After Miss Piggy left, well, things kind of fell apart," he finally admitted, shaking his head. "Fozzie left to pursue his solo career, the band went on tour, and I stayed here to hustle work for everyone else, but, frankly, we haven't had a steady gig since."

"But why did Miss Piggy leave in the first place?" asked Walter.

"That's actually kind of private," Kermit said, turning away. "I'd rather not talk about it."

"Sounds like you guys aren't getting back together anytime soon," Gary admitted.

Mary sighed.

Just when it seemed like everyone had given up, Walter found his voice.

"But, Kermit, don't you understand?" he said.

"You've got to try. The Muppets are amazing! You give people the greatest gift that can ever be given!"

"Children?" Kermit looked confused.

"No." Walter shook his head. "The other one!"

"Lifelong commitment?"

"No! After that!"

Kermit thought for a moment. "Laughter?"

"Yes! The third-greatest gift ever!" Suddenly, Walter was overcome with his love for the Muppets, and he couldn't stop talking. "Your fans never left you! The world hasn't forgotten you! All you have to do is show them."

The frog listened.

"Don't you see, Kermit?" Walter went on. "It's time to play the music."

"It's time to light the lights," Gary added.

"It's time to meet the Muppets," Mary said.

Kermit walked over to the piano and tapped out the rest of the song. "On *The Muppet Show* tonight."

"Please, Kermit," Walter pleaded. "You're my hero."

"Well, I guess we could try," Kermit said finally.

"We?" Walter gulped.

Kermit nodded. "You know, it would be nice to have some moral support."

Walter's jaw dropped. "You mean me? Come with you?"

For the first time in many years, Kermit was excited. And that's a really long time for a frog to go without excitement. "Then it's settled," he said. "Come on! Let's get going! Let's save the Muppet Studios!"

Four

O utside the mansion was an old bronze-colored luxury sedan, chauffeured by Kermit's butler, a robot from the 1980s. Mary had never seen such a beautiful car in all her life; it was everything she could do not to pop the hood and take the engine to pieces. But there wasn't time.

"So, where do we go first?" she asked, leaping into the backseat alongside Gary and Walter. Kermit sat shotgun, next to '80s Robot.

"I have taken the liberty of using my modem to find the Muppets," '80s Robot replied. "Our first destination is Reno, Nevada."

"Who could be in Reno?" Mary whispered, wrinkling her nose.

"I guess we're about to find out," Gary replied, settling in for an adventure.

The car drove along the dreary-looking main strip of Reno, and then pulled up outside a run-down old hotel. The marquee declared a very sorry headline: APPEARING NIGHTLY: THE MOOPETS FEATURING ORIGINAL MUPPETS CAST MEMBER FOZZIE BEAR.

"Oh, man." Walter shook his head. "I do not have a good feeling about this."

If the outside of the hotel was a little less than glamorous, the inside was a downright dump. Up at the front of the room, Fozzie sat on the stage next to someone who looked like Kermit—only not. Gary, Mary, and Walter looked at the real Kermit, at whatever it was on the stage, and then back at Kermit again. Nope, something definitely wasn't quite right about that guy. And he wasn't the only fake on the stage. A Rowlf-esque character was playing piano, and a Piggy-like character was acting as backup singer. So these were the Moopets. Things were rotten in the city of Reno.

Together Fozzie and his band sang a song that sounded a little like Kermit's favorite tune, "Rainbow Connection," but instead of it being about the lovers and the dreamers, it was about room rates and lunch specials. One or two members of the audience applauded quietly, barely managing to put their hands together, as Fozzie made his way wearily offstage. By the stage door, Kermit tapped his old buddy on the shoulder.

"I know, Roowlf, I know I messed up," Fozzie said quickly. "It won't happen again."

"Not Roowlf," Kermit said. "Hi, ho, Fozzie."

The big bear spun around, his mouth wide open. "Kermit?" It was like he couldn't quite believe it. "Kermit! What are you doing here?"

"Great show, Fozzie. It was, um, very informative," Kermit said hesitantly.

"Yeah, it kind of made me want to stay here," Walter added enthusiastically.

"Thanks. I do my best to keep it fresh each night," Fozzie said proudly.

"We need your help, Fozzie." Kermit looked back at Fozzie's bandmates. They did not look nearly as pleased to see him as Fozzie did. "Is there somewhere we can talk?"

"Let's go into my dressing room," Fozzie said with a nod, looking a little scared. "In fact, let's go fast."

He ushered them all through a door labeled FOZZIE BEAR, but instead of walking into a plush dressing room, they found themselves in a dark, dirty alleyway. Sirens sounded, dogs barked, and an old refrigerator buzzed in the background.

"This is…nice?" Kermit tried to find something polite to say, but even the world's most charming frog was at a loss for words.

"Thanks." Fozzie sat on a ratty old couch. "Yeah, the Moopets have all the dressing rooms inside, so this is where I get ready. Sixty-four shows nightly is pretty grueling, so it's nice to have a den to relax in."

"Yeah, airy," Kermit agreed awkwardly.

"Maybe we should give them some space," Mary whispered, dragging Gary away.

"But I want to see what's going to happen," Gary whined. But he could see Mary was right, so the three buddies left the two old friends alone to talk.

"So, what brings you to the entertainment capital of the world?" Fozzie asked over the echoing sirens and alarms and barking dogs.

"Well, an evil oil baron wants to tear down our old Muppet Studios and drill for oil," Kermit declared.

Fozzie sat up straight. "What? No! I mean..." He slouched back on the sofa, trying not to look concerned. "I mean, that's a shame."

"Fozzie," Kermit said, looking down at his flippers, "I'm sorry I haven't been in touch more. I've tried to find work for all of us, but the work dried up after Miss Piggy left, which I kind of blame myself for...."

"It's fine, Kermit," Fozzie said, putting on a brave face. "No need to be in touch. I'm okay. I'm living the dream!"

There would have been an awkward silence between the two, but instead, a loud thunderclap sounded overhead and it began to rain.

"Not again!" Fozzie wailed. "Save the cushions! They were from Ma!"

Kermit didn't mind the rain, but he did mind what was happening to his friend. "I'm so sorry, Fozzie. If I'd known you were here, in this place..."

"It's not your fault," the bear replied. "We had a good run."

"Well, I don't know, I just..." Kermit didn't quite know what to say. He had been sure Fozzie would want to help. "That place has a lot of senti-mental value, and I just thought if we all got together for one last show, maybe we could raise enough money to buy it back."

"I don't know, Kermit." Fozzie didn't look con-vinced. "We haven't done our act together in years. What if everyone watches and we fail? What if no one watches and we fail?"

"That's a chance we have to take." Kermit looked determined. It was an odd expression on a frog, but it was plain to see that he meant it.

"I've spent years building my solo career," Fozzie said, but Kermit could tell he was wavering. "And my new showbiz family loves me...."

As if on cue, Roowlf Moopet stuck his head around the door. "Fozzie, what the heck are you doing? Hibernating?" he barked. "Our next show is in thirty seconds. We hired you, we can fire you! Foozie the Moopet is just waiting for our call!"

Fozzie looked at the Moopet. Then he looked at Kermit. He immediately made up his mind.

"Okay, maybe you're right," Fozzie cried as he jumped to his feet and bolted for the end of the alley with Kermit tucked under one arm. "Let's go!"

For the next Muppet pickup, '80s Robot drove them to a giant, shiny skyscraper. It reached up high into the sky, dwarfing all the surrounding buildings. Walter thought whoever was inside must be a billionaire. But who?

"Whoa," he breathed. "It can't be?"

"I think so." Gary pointed toward a statue in front of the building. It depicted a dignified figure, nobly holding a plunger: the artist formerly known as The Great Gonzo.

"Yep," Kermit confirmed. "According to '80s Robot, he's the richest plumbing magnate in the world."

"I'm sure he's still the same old crazy Gonzo," Walter tried to convince Kermit and himself.

The inside of the building was gigantic, filled with busy workers. The gang sat nervously on the edge of the sofa, waiting for their appointment with Mr. Gonzo. Fozzie couldn't stop staring at all the employees, and Walter concentrated on not fainting again. Kermit gulped, preparing his speech. Suddenly they heard a raspy voice coming down the corridor.

"Order twenty thousand tons of plumbers' putty from Beijing, and send back the twenty thousand tons of the kid stuff," the voice commanded. "And cancel the order of real snakes to replace drain snakes. Apparently real snakes need oxygen."

Gonzo entered the room, surrounded by workers, who were taking notes of every word he said.

"Oh, and a memo to the waterless-toilet department: I don't care about the mess—keep trying...."
He reached his desk and saw the Muppets waiting

for him. Without blinking, he nodded briefly. "You have thirty seconds," he said. "Go."

"Gonzo, it's us!" Kermit couldn't believe the changes in his old friend. This guy was hardly about to shoot himself out of a cannon. "We need to talk! I don't know quite how to say this, but it would appear that—"

"Don't forget to mention about the oil baron," Fozzie interrupted.

"Fozzie!" Kermit said, pointing at a countdown clock on Gonzo's desk. "I was about to! Could you give me a moment?"

"Just remember to tell him about the evil oil baron," Fozzie repeated.

"I'm going to!"

"Evil oil baron."

"Fozzie!"

The timer ran out and Gonzo turned his back. Fozzie held his hat in his hands and hung his head.

"Oops." He laughed awkwardly. "Sorry."

"Time's up. Thank you, guys," Gonzo said in a cold, hard voice. "If there's anything I can do, be sure to let one of my people know."

Fozzie put up his hand. "I've always wanted one of those Japanese toilets."

"That's not why we're here!" Kermit glared at Fozzie. "We need to get the old gang back together, Gonzo!"

Gonzo stared wistfully out the window. "I'm sorry, but I've put away childish things," he said, pressing his fingers lightly against the glass. "The world of plumbing needs me. My answer is no. Good day."

Suddenly, Walter stepped forward. "I just want to say, when I was a kid, I once saw you recite *Hamlet* while riding a motorcycle through a flaming hoop, and it made me feel like I could do anything... and so you'll always be great to *me*."

But Gonzo appeared unmoved.

One by one, the group filed out of the room, heartbroken. What would they do without Gonzo?

Once his old friends had left, Gonzo let out a huge sigh.

"Cluck cluck cluck?" Camilla, Gonzo's girl-friend and confidante, stared at him.

"No," he replied, "I'm not sure."

Kermit and the gang were climbing back into the car with heavy hearts when a loud scream rang out from the very top of Gonzo's skyscraper. Way up high they could just make out a figure, tearing off a business suit and holding what looked like a chicken.

"Wait, you guys!" Gonzo wailed. "I've been wearing this under my suit every single day for years!" Shedding his shirt and tie, he revealed his signature silver jumpsuit with the lightning bolt on the front. "Look out below!"

Kermit covered his eyes—he just couldn't watch. Gonzo leapt from the top of the building in a spectacular spiral, Camilla in one hand, a remote control in the other, and crash-landed right on top of his statue.

"Attention citizens of Earth!" he cried, dangling from the statue's nose. "The Great Gonzo is back! Before you all, I pledge never to hold a plunger again!"

With that, he pressed a big red button on the remote control. A great rumble came from the skyscraper and people began spilling out onto the street. Seconds later, the entire building exploded, crashing to the ground in a huge cloud of dust.

"That was an expensive-looking explosion...." Fozzie pushed Gonzo and Camilla into the car. "Let's go!"

"Man, I missed you guys," Gonzo exclaimed, hugging everyone in the car. "That was great. So, what was the problem again?"

"Tex Richman is going to buy the Muppet Studios and tear it to the ground to drill for oil if we can't raise ten million dollars," Kermit explained. "So we're going to stage a comeback show!"

"Why didn't you say so?" Gonzo laughed. "I'm super rich! All my money is right there, back in the building...."

Gonzo stared at the smoking remains of his sky-scraper. Everyone stared at Gonzo.

"Sorry about that."

"So, who's up next?" Gary asked as the car slowed to a halt next to what looked like a swanky resort complex.

"Who do you think?" Kermit took a deep breath and hopped out of the car to point at a sign. It wasn't a resort at all. It was a celebrity anger-management center. "I think I'm going to need all you guys. Come on."

Through the window, Walter spotted Animal, calmly sitting in a circle of celebrities. There wasn't a trace of his trademark anarchy in his eyes, and he rocked back and forth in his chair.

"Animal," a woman holding a clipboard at the head of the room addressed the Muppet. "How are you feeling?"

"In...control," Animal replied serenely.

The moderator looked pleased. "Good. Now, who's next?"

Before any of the assembled actors, models, or singers could reply, Animal spotted his friends at the door and began to tremble.

"Animal!" Kermit waved from the doorway. "Um, I was wondering if I could talk to you?"

"We're having a meeting here, man," piped up one of the famous actors. "You're being rude, frog."

"We're getting the Muppets back together, and we need you to drum again," Walter yelled. He still got a little overexcited when he saw one of his heroes for the first time.

"B-back together?" Animal stammered. "Ani-Animal drum? AYAYAY!"

"Hey, don't use the *D* word, man," the actor said, standing in front of Animal. "It's his trigger word. You want to talk to Animal, you come through me. I'm his sponsor."

"It's just really important that they get their drum—" Gary began to explain the Muppets' plight, but the actor wasn't listening. Instead, he socked Gary right in the chops.

"And it's *my* trigger word as well!" The actor bounced up and down on the spot. Mary put up her fists—no one punched her Gary!

"Hey, buddy," another actor said, tapping Animal's sponsor on the shoulder. "We talked about this on Tuesday, remember?"

" 'Tuesday' is another one of my trigger words!" yelled the first actor. Then a huge fight broke out, with Animal in the middle. The moderator crouched under a table, fending off angry famous people with her clipboard.

"Come on, Animal," Kermit said, grabbing his friend and pulling him out the door. "Let's get you out of here!"

Five

After a whirlwind tour of Arctic wastelands, a desert, a jungle, and even the 1970s, they'd collected Rowlf, Sweetums, Dr. Bunsen Honeydew and Beaker, Swedish Chef, and Dr. Teeth and The Electric Mayhem. The car was pretty full. At last, the Muppets were back together. Well, almost.

"Looks like we've got everyone," Kermit said, clapping his hands together. "Let's start planning the telethon! We've got ten million dollars to raise."

"Not everyone, Kermit," Fozzie said, looking around the car.

"Nope." Kermit stared straight ahead. "We've got everyone."

"Where's—?" Mary began.

"All done here!" Kermit cut her off quickly.

"Miss—" Gary tried.

"All good!" Kermit yelled.

"Piggy?" Walter finished the question on everyone's lips.

Kermit scrunched up his face.

"Kermit? We're going to get Miss Piggy, right?" Fozzie asked.

A murmur ran through the car. Surely they weren't going to perform without the pig?

"Okay," Kermit relented. "We'll go and get Miss Piggy." But he knew this was not going to be easy. He hadn't spoken to her since she moved to Paris, all those years ago....

Miss Piggy wasn't just a pig in Paris. She was *the* pig in Paris. Since retiring from the Muppets, she had become the editor in chief of the world's most famous fashion magazine. A snobby-looking assistant guarded the door of Piggy's sleek office.

"Hi, ho," Kermit began. He was nervous. "We're here to see the editor. It's urgent?"

The assistant didn't even look up from her computer. "She has an opening in early September."

"That's a really long time away! We said it was urgent!" Fozzie really wasn't getting the message. "What're we supposed to do between now and then?"

The assistant threw him a look that suggested she had some great ideas about what he could do.

"She won't see you without an appointment," she said eventually.

"Let me take care of this," Gary said, pushing to the front. He gave the assistant a huge smile and then said in a low voice, "Please, please, please, it'll be really embarrassing for me now if you don't let us in. Seriously, I'm begging you."

The assistant looked at him in the same way she might look at something that was stuck to the sole of her shoe.

"No."

Mary sighed. "Sometimes only a lady knows how to do something," she said quietly to Walter. "A little manners go a long way...."

"Just because you said that quietly doesn't mean I didn't hear you," the assistant said pointedly in Mary's direction. "The answer is still no."

Miserable and tired, the gang stood outside the offices of Piggy's magazine. What were they supposed to do now?

"Yes!" Fozzie grinned as a tall man in a suit pushed past them into the building. It had given him an idea. "Muppet Man!"

"What's a Muppet man?" Walter asked.

Five minutes later, he really wished he hadn't asked.

The Muppets were all crammed inside a man's suit, with Fozzie's head sticking out the top.

"Someone's put on a few extra pounds since we last did this," a voice huffed from somewhere around the left hip.

"And your butt hasn't gotten any smaller," another voice wailed from the left leg.

"Quiet, guys." Fozzie presented himself to Piggy's receptionist. He coughed and spoke in a deep voice with a very, very strange accent. "I have an appointment to see the editor."

"Okay then," the assistant said, standing up and waving them into the office.

Everything was stylish, ultramodern, and fashion forward. And sitting in the middle of it all, staring out the window at the Eiffel Tower while chomping on a cinnamon bun, was Miss Piggy.

"Mademoiselle Cochonnet?" The assistant knocked for her boss's attention. "This gentleman says he has an appointment."

"Send him in." Piggy dismissed her minion and

stared at Muppet Man. "You look awfully familiar," she said with narrowed eyes.

"So do you," Fozzie said, in the same fake accent he'd used on the assistant.

Before Piggy could reply, Muppet Man's leg began to shake uncontrollably.

"Message to the head!" Gonzo yelled. "Left leg going down! Left leg going down!"

"What?" Piggy shrieked as a pile of Muppets exploded from inside the suit. "I can't believe I fell for Muppet Man!"

The Muppets dusted themselves off and found their feet. Piggy was furious. She wanted to scream, she wanted to karate-chop someone, she wanted to— And then she saw him. Her prince, her *petit grenouille*, her Kermie.

"Kermit?" She pressed a hand to her face.

"Hello, Piggy."

Before she could stop herself, Piggy launched

herself across the room and began covering Kermit in kisses.

It was as if the wedding had been yesterday....

Kermit had looked so handsome as they had said their vows, even if he did look a little confused.

"I thought Gonzo was going to play the priest?" he had asked.

Piggy, in her beautiful wedding dress, had only laughed nervously, said her vows, and then closed her eyes while the frog kissed her. The crowd went nuts and she had never been so happy.

A couple of weeks later, Piggy had rushed into Kermit's office, clutching a black-and-white wedding photo.

"Kermie!" She waved the picture at him. "Our first photo as a married couple!"

Kermit dropped his head to his desk. They had been through this over and over again. The wedding had just been a scene they filmed for a movie. "Piggy, we're not really married!" he reminded her. "You need a *real* priest to be…" And then the penny dropped as Kermit put two and two together. Gonzo had been cast as the priest, but some other guy had played the part. And that other guy wasn't an actor—he was a real priest! So he had really married them!

"Oh, no," he said. "You didn't?"

"I'm so happy," Piggy carried on talking as though she couldn't hear her husband. "Let's share our joy with ten of the world's leading publications!"

She threw open the door to a pack of paparazzi, flashbulbs popping everywhere.

"Kermit!" one shouted. "How does it feel to be married?"

"Kermit!" bellowed another. "Are you going to move into the house Piggy has built for you?"

"Piggy!" Kermit yelled over the journalists at the door. "I thought the wedding was just part of the show?"

The pig paused and frowned. "But aren't you happy?"

"You're supposed to *ask* someone before you marry them!" Kermit was getting mad. Madder than a frog should ever get. "Not *trick* them! Why must you always pull stunts like this? This is the last straw!"

"Oh, Kermie." Piggy smiled and sighed happily. "Our first argument as a married couple."

The frog had taken all he could take, and he could take no more. "You're fired!" he shouted. "Fired, fired, fired!"

Piggy gasped. "You can't replace me."

"Watch me," Kermit replied.

"But I'm your wife!" The pig was shocked. What was he saying?

"You're NOT my wife!" Kermit flapped his arms angrily, panting. "You'll never, ever, *ever* be my wife!"

For the first time in Muppet history, Miss Piggy fell silent. She stared at Kermit as a tear trickled down her cheek. Then she held up the photo from their faux wedding and tore it in two. Before Kermit could say another word, she turned on her heels and flounced out of the office.

"Wait!" Kermit called. He knew he'd gone too far, been too harsh. But it was too late. She was gone....

"Wow," Mary whispered to Gary back in the office. "That was a very informative flashback."

"No!" Miss Piggy tore herself away from the little green love of her life. "I promised myself I'd never go back. I am woman. I am strong. You must leave. At once! *Dépêche-toi!*"

"All right, we tried," Kermit said, way too fast for Piggy's liking.

"Wait!" Walter turned to Miss Piggy. "You don't know me, but I'm your biggest fan. We need you to come with us to L.A. The Muppet Studios is in danger."

"Our studio?" Piggy said. "In danger? Kermie, is this true?"

"It's true," Kermit confirmed. "We need to put on the show again."

Miss Piggy looked at her assembled friends, together again after so many years.

"Before I decide anything," she announced, "I need to talk to you alone, frog. *Moi et toi.*"

Kermit gulped. "Sure, Piggy."

"Just give me one teensy second." Piggy batted her lashes at the other Muppets. "I just need to make a very important call. If you'll all excuse me?"

The Muppets whooped happily as they left Piggy's office... well, all were happy except Kermit. Slamming the door behind them, Miss Piggy began to hyperventilate. The only cure for which was to bang her head repeatedly on her desk.

"Keep it together, pig!" she bellowed at herself. "He's just a frog. Like any other frog. God, I'm drenched in sweat. Cover-up time!"

She pulled open a drawer and doused herself in

scented powder and perfume. How was she supposed to deal with Kermit?

Outside, Mary and Gary decided to take a stroll in the Parisian sunshine. It wasn't every day they were in France. It was only when they reached the Eiffel Tower that Mary realized that it was exactly like her dream!

"Mary?" She turned around to see Gary reaching into his jacket pocket. This was it! He was going to propose!

"Oh, Gary!" She had never been so excited in all her life. Finally, all her wishes were coming true—

"Will you take a photo of me and Walter?" Gary handed her his camera.

Mary's heart sank. Of course. Walter.

"Sure," she said with a sad smile. "Pass it here."

She took some silly shots of the best friends and

handed the camera back to Gary. He didn't ask for a picture with her. Mary tried to be happy, but it was hard. Would things ever change?

On the other side of Paris, where the sun had already gone down, Piggy and Kermit strolled down the banks of the River Seine.

"The past is the past," Piggy said dramatically, as if she were in an old movie. "What's meant to be was meant to be."

"Memories are good, but they can also be a prison," replied Kermit.

"A prison of our own making," Piggy acknowledged.

"Okay, Piggy." Enough was enough with the fancy talk. "The last time I saw you, I said some things I regret."

"No, you spoke the truth," she corrected him. "You never intended to marry me, even after I built us a house where we would raise tadpoles and grow old together."

"Who do you think has been taking care of that house all these years?" Kermit asked. Piggy froze. He had been looking after their love nest?

"I just don't know why you have to be so... flamboyant all the time." Kermit sighed. This was never going to be easy.

"I play to the audience, Kermit. My audience." Piggy sighed dramatically—as if she could sigh any other way. "Why can't you accept that about me? Why must you try to change who I am?"

"Piggy," Kermit said. "I didn't come here to talk about the past. This is bigger than just you and me. It's about the whole gang!"

"That's just it! It *is* about me and you!" She paused for dramatic effect. She wasn't giving in.

"What are we going to do without you?" Kermit gasped.

Piggy sighed. "It's always *we*, isn't it?" She began to walk away sadly, her decision made.

"But Piggy!" Kermit protested.

She looked back over her shoulder, her long blond hair blowing in the breeze. "I should warn you," she said, pouting, "I'm not easily replaced."

The Muppets were all staring out the window of the car, waiting to see what would happen. A mix of gasps, sighs, and whispers sounded as Kermit slouched back up the avenue alone.

"What happened?" Fozzie asked. "Where is she?"

"She's not coming." Kermit climbed into the front seat sadly.

"But we always do the show together," Fozzie went on. "We're a family!"

"We'll come up with something else," Kermit said in a tired voice.

"But—" Fozzie started to argue, but Mary rested a hand on his furry arm and shook her head. Everyone was quiet. As they left Paris, Kermit sighed and stared out into the night.

Across the City of Lights, Piggy sighed, too, as she opened a drawer and gazed at a picture of herself and Kermit in happier times.

It took a little while for Kermit to come up with a replacement for Miss Piggy, but he did it.

"What's everyone so sad about?" Miss Poogy the Moopet said from the backseat. "Jeez."

"K-Kermit?" stammered Fozzie. "Are you sure this is a good idea?"

"Sure." Kermit nodded with an almost convincing smile. "It'll work out fine. Now let's start rehearsing."

The Muppets burst into song for the first time in years. And they were awful. No one knew when to come in, the harmonies were off, and most of them couldn't remember the words. Gary looked at Walter. The Muppets were back. But they were bad.

"Will you guys give it a rest?" barked Miss

Poogy. "You have totally lost it. I mean, this is embarrassing right now. Have some dignity."

No one wanted to admit it, but the Moopet had a point.

"Hey." Gonzo elbowed Fozzie. "Miss Piggy hasn't changed a bit!"

Back in Los Angeles, Tex Richman was reading the newspaper, and he did not like what he saw. The headline read MUPPETS REUNITE FOR POSSIBLE BENEFIT CONCERT! A shadow that had nothing to do with his large ten-gallon hat crossed over his face.

"Well, gentlemen," he said, steepling his fingers under his chin. "It would appear we have some potential competition on the Muppet property. The paper says they've gotten back together again."

Uncle Deadly the Dragon pricked up his ears. "The Muppets got back together?" He sounded altogether too excited for Tex's liking. "That reminds me of a song...."

"No singing!" Tex barked. "This is a workplace, not some Broadway revue."

Deadly quickly apologized. He did not want to be on the wrong side of Tex's temper.

"No matter. The point is, I don't care who or what reunited. That studio and oil belong to me... and, of course, my shareholders," Tex said, giving the shareholders who were in the room a slick grin. "Bring me a copy of the standard rich-and-famous contract. I've got homework to do. If it's a fight they want, a fight they'll get. They're going to run with their tails between their legs. Literally. For those with tails. Maniacal laugh, maniacal laugh, maniacal laugh."

"Why does he do that?" one of the other hench-men whispered to Uncle Deadly. "You have to admit, it's a little odd."

"Because he's never laughed," the dragon

explained. "Nothing has ever made him laugh. Not even the Muppets are funny to him."

"Who thinks the Muppets are funny?" Tex bellowed across the room. "Do you want to be fired?"

Uncle Deadly cowered in the corner. Yep, anyone who didn't find the Muppets funny definitely had something seriously wrong with them.

While Tex was not laughing about the Muppets, the Muppets were worrying about pitching their TV special to the networks. So far, every TV station in town had turned them down. This network was their last shot.

Veronica, a cutthroat young executive, sat back in her chair after Kermit's pitch. She didn't look too impressed.

"Listen, Kermit," she said. "I like you. I was a fan when I was a kid, but I'm gonna shoot straight. You guys aren't famous anymore."

"I wish she'd shot a little more curvy," Fozzie said, pulling at his bow tie. "Wocka! Wocka!"

The exec did the only thing she could and ignored him. "The answer is no. You're not cynical or violent—kids can't relate to you. My top two shows right now are *Punch Teacher* and *Credit Card Club*. That's what kids want today."

She showed the Muppets clips of both shows. Kermit gulped. This was what kids were watching on TV?

"You're no longer relevant," Veronica declared.

The Muppets hung their heads. After everything they'd gone through to come back together, they'd failed. Tex was going to get his hands on the Muppet Studios after all.

"Before I go," Kermit piped up from the doorway, "well, there's just something I want to say. I think kids are smarter and better than all this junk. Sure, they'll watch this stuff if you don't offer anything else, but we have a chance to make this world better and more fun!"

He drew himself up on his little froggy legs while Veronica leaned forward. She was really listening.

"You're not going to do that by filling their heads with violence or materialism. You're gonna do that through laughter and friendship and hope. I know we're not famous anymore, but I think you're making a big mistake." He nodded sadly, preparing to leave.

"Wait!" Veronica shouted. "You're right!"

Kermit stopped in his tracks. At last! Someone who understood!

"I am?"

"Yes." Veronica smiled. "You're not famous."

"Oh." Kermit's shoulders dropped. That was about all the disappointment he could take.

Just as he and the rest of the Muppets were about to leave, the door flew open and a panicked-looking junior executive rushed into the room.

"Veronica, disaster!" he panted. "*Punch Teacher*

is being sued by the Teachers' Association of America. We have no show this week."

"What's their problem?" Veronica groaned. "Where am I going to find a hundred and twenty minutes of programming on such short notice?"

Kermit coughed loudly. It was a heck of a coincidence, but he wasn't complaining.

"Good news, Muppets," Veronica said grudgingly. "You've got yourselves a show."

The Muppets went nuts.

"No going nuts in my office," she yelled. "The carpet is new. Now, there's one condition. You need a celebrity host or the show is canceled, okay?"

While the other Muppets dashed outside, where they could go nuts without destroying Veronica's shag carpet, Kermit tried not to hear Veronica's closing words as a threat. Find a celebrity host in three days? *Gulp.*

Seven

"Can you believe it?" Walter said the next day. "We're actually inside the Muppet Theater!"

He stared around in awe. Gary and Mary wondered if they were seeing the same thing as their friend. The theater was in ruins. The seats were all torn up, the backdrops were all broken, none of the lights worked, and the curtains were all ripped. And that was just what they could *see*.

"It smells weird in here," Miss Poogy pointed out gruffly. "Jeez, did something die? If anyone needs me, I'll be in the pig's old dressing room, taking a nap."

Really, no one was okay with Miss Piggy's replacement, but they were all too terrified of her to say anything. Miss Piggy was hardly docile, but Poogy was just begging for a fight.

Once everyone was seated in the auditorium (everyone but Poogy, of course), Kermit took his place at the podium for the first time in years. It was almost too much for Walter to bear. He was so excited to be with his heroes, in their theater!

"Okay, gee, well, welcome back, everybody!" Kermit cheered and nodded at his old Muppet family. "It's so great to see all your faces again. We're back together, all of us. Well, nearly all of us. Now, I know the old place doesn't look its best, but don't worry. It'll be fine. We always come through for each other when the chips are down."

"But Kermit, there's no way we can rehearse with the place in this state," Fozzie said, gesturing around the run-down old theater.

"Don't say another word!" Gary leapt to his feet. "Mary, Walter, and I are happy to help rebuild your theater! It'd be an honor for all of us."

Mary looked startled. "Gary, wait," she said quietly. "What about our vacation? And our dinner on Friday?"

"We'll still have it. I promise," he said with such a kind look on his face that Mary couldn't help but melt. "It's just, well, you teach shop! You could help repair this place."

"A shop teacher! Boy! We could really use you. Please, Mary?" Kermit pleaded.

"Well, in that case, of course I'd be happy to," Mary said, relenting. She really did want to help the Muppets. "Show me what you need."

"And I can help clean up with Walter," Gary added.

"Yeah," Walter agreed. He couldn't remember a time he'd felt so happy. "We'll have this place ship-shape in no time!"

The Muppets all cheered.

It took everyone's best efforts to get the theater back in shape. Mary and Sweetums worked together to repair the balcony so that Statler and Waldorf had a home again. Swedish Chef cleared the old kitchen—with the help of a flamethrower. And Fozzie cleaned the floor with Walter. Yes, actually *with* Walter: He used his new pal as a mop. Gary watched from a distance. He was so happy to see Walter so happy, but it was weird to see him, well, *so* happy. Gary was just so used to being Walter's best friend, he felt a little left out....

Backstage, the others began work on the dressing room. Fozzie found a handful of old headshots in a drawer.

"Can you believe this old hairdo?" He slapped his hand across his eyes. "What was I thinking? Totally ridiculous!"

He held the photo up for everyone to see.

"Uh, Fozzie?" Gonzo rested on his broom. "You look exactly the same."

By the end of the day, the auditorium was clean again. Everyone was exhausted.

"Let's call it a day," Kermit announced just as everyone was about to collapse. "We start rehearsal tomorrow, nine AM sharp!"

"See you tomorrow, Kermit!" Gary called happily. He was just about the only one with any energy left. "Walter and I are pretty handy with a needle and thread. We'll get those costumes ready in no time."

Mary jogged down the aisle to catch up with him on his way out the door. She was covered in dust and grime and looked like she was ready to fall down, she was so tired.

"We're helping again tomorrow?" she asked. "I was thinking we could go to the beach, or see the Hollywood sign?"

"We've got plenty of time," Gary said, patting her on the shoulder. "These guys need us."

"Well, we've helped quite a lot," Mary pointed out. "And we haven't done anything on our GARY AND MARY'S THINGS TO DO IN L.A. list."

She pulled the list out of her pocket and showed him that every single item had an unchecked box beside it.

Gary didn't get it. Why didn't Mary understand? "Walter needs me!" he explained.

They both looked over to where Walter was merrily chatting away with the Muppets. He spotted his friends leaving and gave them a cheery wave. Then Walter went right back to talking to Kermit and the others. He looked so happy.

"I'm not sure he does," Mary said, shrugging.

"Well, I think he does," Gary huffed. "And I want to come back here with my best friend to make sure he's okay. I'm sorry."

Now Mary was mad. Why couldn't Gary see that Walter was happier with the Muppets? They didn't need to be joined at the hip anymore.

"I'm sorry, too," she said. "But I'm here on vacation, and starting tomorrow I'm having one. You can stay here or come with me. I'll leave it up to you."

And with that, she pushed past him and stomped out of the theater.

Gary watched, perplexed. He was pretty sure she was annoyed about something... but what?

That night, the Muppets were all sleeping soundly in the theater. Statler and Waldorf snoozed away in their pj's up in the balcony. Only Kermit and Fozzie lay awake in their hammocks.

"Kermit?" Fozzie whispered.

"Yes, Fozzie?" the frog replied.

"We'll be okay, right?" Fozzie asked. "We

It's a musical send-off from Smalltown, USA, as Gary, Mary, and Walter set out for Hollywood!

Picture-perfect buddies Gary and Walter have been lifelong best friends.

What evil lurks? Tex Richman and his henchmen do the most evil of deeds: paperwork!

The plot thickens! Walter overhears Tex's plan.

The gang gets back together!
It's time to get things started!

The triumphant return of world-famous daredevil
and performance artist Gonzo the Great!

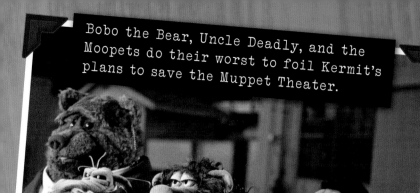

Bobo the Bear, Uncle Deadly, and the Moopets do their worst to foil Kermit's plans to save the Muppet Theater.

A world-class diva, Miss Piggy isn't going to let anyone—let alone this imposter Moopet, Miss Poogy—take her place. Outta her way: It's showtime!

Fozzie cleans up the Muppet Theater with Walter—literally!

Mary and Gary help, and Rizzo skates by!

Piggy and Kermit shared a dramatic moment long ago...

...but can they work together again?

Walter, his BFF Gary, and his BFF's girlfriend, Mary, are ready to help the Muppets save their theater.

haven't done this for a long time...and I really don't want to go back to Reno...."

"We'll be fine," Kermit tried to reassure his old friend. "Look how we cleaned up today! Same old pulling together."

"I guess you're right," Fozzie said with a smile. "Thanks, buddy. Night-night."

Listening to Fozzie drifting off into rubber-chicken dreams, Kermit stared up at the ceiling, trying to believe his own words. They would be fine. Better than fine!

They had to be.

Eight

The next morning Gary opened his eyes, happy as a clam and ready for another day of work with Walter and Mary, but when he rolled over, Mary was nowhere to be seen. She'd already left the hotel.

"Huh." Gary sat up, confused. And then he remembered the last thing she had said to him: She was going to have a vacation whether he came along or not. It looked like she wasn't joking. Suddenly Gary wasn't as happy as a clam. Unless clams were generally miserable.

Arriving at the Muppet Theater didn't make him feel any better. Things were just not going well.

"Anyone got some kerosene?" Poogy appeared from backstage, clutching an armful of Miss Piggy's costumes. "Thought I'd take these old pig dresses out back and burn 'em."

The Muppets all gasped.

Suddenly, there was a knock at the door. A Miss Piggy–shaped silhouette appeared, and everyone gasped again.

"Vegetariana pizza for Gonzo?"

It was just a pizza delivery guy wearing huge headphones. Poogy cackled and dumped Miss Piggy's dresses on the floor.

"Hold it right there, sausage snout!" The pizza guy stepped to one side to reveal someone else in the doorway. It was the real Miss Piggy!

"Look what the cat dragged in!" Poogy snarled. "Sorry, Miss Piggy, but you've been replaced. Permanently."

The Moopet pulled out a pair of brass knuckles while Piggy prepared her best martial-arts moves. The Muppets gathered around. This was about to get ugly.

But before Poogy could even make a move, with a loud "HII-YAH!" Piggy launched herself in a flying karate kick and knocked Poogy across the room.

"Too bad I'm irreplaceable!" Piggy screeched. The Muppets all rushed to hug her, but Miss Piggy only had eyes for one amphibian. But he wasn't there.

"You guys stink!" Poogy said, pushing herself up off the floor. "Good luck saving your crappy theater—you're gonna need it."

No one was watching as she limped out of the Muppet Theater. They were too busy observing Kermit, who had just appeared in front of Piggy.

"Er, hi," he said. "It's good to see you."

"I'm not here for you." Piggy sniffed and tossed her head. "I'm here for 'we.'"

"Okay, Piggy." Kermit looked a little crestfallen, but he didn't have time to be sad. There was too much to do. "Okay, everybody, let's start rehearsals!"

Beginning at the beginning, the Muppets were trying to sing their signature song, but nothing felt right. With Animal having taken up the triangle in place of the rock-and-roll drums, the others couldn't keep time. It was not time to start the music, and it was most certainly not time to light the lights. What had become of *The Muppet Show*?

"Let's just start rehearsing the acts," Kermit called out in the midst of the Muppet-y chaos. "We'll come back to the song. Fozzie, you're up!"

The bear took the stage with a huge grin. "What's the bear capital of the world?" He paused for the audience. "Mos-*cow*! No, that's not right. New *Pork* City! No, that's not it, either...."

Kermit held his head in his hands. "We'll come back to you, too. Who's next?"

Gonzo and Camilla graced the stage. "The Great Gonzo needs a fearless human volunteer," he announced. Gary put his hand up excitedly. Oh, boy—he was going to be part of Gonzo's act!

Gonzo sat Gary on a stool and carefully placed a bowling pin on his head.

"No!" Kermit leapt to his feet. "Not the bowling-ball trick!"

But it was too late. Gonzo swung a bowling ball in a circular motion, spinning around and around and around. Everyone looked away; this never ended well. But apparently there was a first time for everything. Gonzo released the ball and it flew through the air, knocking the pin off the first time, barely disturbing a hair on Gary's head. Everyone clapped, in complete shock.

"You're welcome!" Gonzo bowed deeply.

"Yes, you're welcome," Dr. Bunsen Honeydew said, appearing from the wings. "My hyperintelligent remote-controlled bowling ball was programmed with zero margin for error."

Gonzo blushed. As much as it was possible for a blue weirdo to blush.

"Um, Doctor, did you say zero margin for error?" Kermit asked. The ball had risen into the air and was floating a few feet away from Dr. Honeydew's head.

"Yes," he confirmed. "That is, of course, unless the ball achieved sentience and began to think for itself. But there is less than a point-zero-zero-zero-zero-one percent chance of that occurring."

"Um, Doctor?" Kermit pointed toward the floating ball.

The scientist turned just in time to see the ball zoom toward his head.

"It has achieved sentience!" Bunsen wailed. "Run for your lives! Save the women and children!"

But since the ball appeared to be interested only in walloping its maker, and the Muppets needed all the practice they could get, Kermit went on with the rehearsals instead.

"Gonzo, the Muppets are about artistic integrity, not cheap tricks!" Kermit yelled. "Next!"

Fozzie took to the stage. "I'm back with something new!" He pointed to his feet. "Fart shoes! Patent pending." With each step he took, his shoes made an unfortunate noise.

"Good grief," Kermit said, waving him off the stage. "Who's next?"

Then Kermit spotted Walter over in a corner, merrily mending costumes.

"Hey, Walter," he called. "We really need some help. Do you think you could perform your talent for us?"

Walter gulped. His talent? Perform? With the Muppets?

"I don't have a talent," he mumbled. "Really, I'm just happy helping out."

"Everyone has a talent, Walter," Kermit said, placing a hand on his new friend's arm. "Will you do it for me?"

"I—I need some time to practice." He gulped. "Then I'll do it."

"Okay." Kermit smiled. "Let's see who's left."

Fozzie looked at the rehearsal running sheet. "It's just your duet with Piggy, Kermit."

"I'm not sure that's a good idea," Kermit said, stalling. That was the last thing he needed right now—a show full of bad acts *and* a concussion.

"C'mon, Kermit." Fozzie wasn't giving up. "For the show."

"Okay." Kermit resigned himself to the duet, and to the possibility of Piggy's wrath. He started a slow and steady journey to Miss Piggy's dressing room.

"Hey, Piggy?" he said cautiously, hiding behind the door. "It's time to rehearse our duet."

"Oh, Kermie." Piggy opened the door fully, already dressed for their number. And in the middle of rehearsal with Pepe the King Prawn. "I actually have a new duet partner. Nothing personal."

"Of course." Kermit was shocked. And sad. And shocked at how sad he was. But he walked away. "No problem, Piggy."

"Thanks, Kermie," she called, taking a few steps back and returning her attention to her duet partner. Her tiny, shrimp duet partner. "Now, Pepe, time to try the lift again!"

Life didn't get any easier for Kermit on his way back to the stage. Veronica, the network executive, was waiting for him with her arms folded. She did not look very happy.

"There you are," she snapped. Nope, not happy at all.

"Veronica! Great to see you. Can I get you anything?"

"The show is a disaster, frog," she said, glaring at him. "Who's hosting on the night?"

"Well, um, uh..." Kermit looked around for help. "Me?"

"Adorable." Veronica gave him a sweet smile.

Then she snarled. Actually snarled, like made the noise and everything. "No way. You need a celebrity. Find one before Saturday or you're canceled."

"How are we going to do that?" Kermit began to panic. "We only have a couple of days! It's impossible!"

"Not my problem, frog," Veronica said on her way out. "Challenges only make you stronger."

Back onstage, the Muppets were freaking out.

"What if we don't have *it* anymore?" Fozzie wailed. "Maybe we've lost *it*?"

"Okay, listen up, everybody," Kermit said, then took a deep breath. This wasn't the worst idea ever, was it? "Let's go ask this Tex Richman for our studio back. I'm sure he's a reasonable guy."

Tex Richman was not a reasonable guy.

"Which is why, in conclusion, we humbly ask

that you give us back the studio," Kermit explained to him. "It sure would mean a lot to us. What do you say?"

Tex sat back in his chair and stared at the Muppets.

"What do I say?" he said as he took in the whole motley crew. The frog, the pig, the bear, the dog, whatever that blue weirdo was. Pathetic. "What I say is, I'm rich. Which means I am better than you. And it means I can do whatever I want, whenever I want."

The Muppets all took a small step backward.

"I hate you, Muppets. I've always hated you," Tex went on. "Ever since I was a little boy, everyone laughed at everything you did. But not me. And then everyone laughed at me, for not laughing at you! So now, Muppets, I get the last laugh."

Everyone waited for him to laugh.

"So to speak," he said. "I can't laugh!"

"That doesn't seem fair," Kermit replied. "It's not our fault that you don't know how to laugh, Mr. Richman."

Maybe he couldn't laugh, but he was more than capable of a sickening grin. "Well, I'm afraid I've only just started." He pulled out the standard rich-and-famous contract. "You didn't read this contract too well. Not only did you sign away the studios, you included the character and performance rights to the Muppets. Kermit the lovable frog, Miss Piggy the arrogant pig—"

"Watch it, turtleneck!" Piggy bristled.

"Anyway, I already got buyers for your names." Tex smiled as the door opened to reveal Poogy and the rest of the Moopets.

"Told you I'd be back. Well, now I am. Back," Poogy said. "Darn it, I practiced that, like, a bunch of times, and I still got it wrong."

The Muppets were shocked. And more than a little bit scared.

"You're relics!" Tex shouted. "A hippy-dippy, goody-goody singing-dancing act. No one cares anymore."

The Muppets all looked at one another. Surely he wasn't right? Surely people still cared?

"Bye, Muppets," Tex called as he waved the gang out of his office. "Better start thinking of some new names." The Muppets couldn't believe it. Tex Richman would even own their *names*!

"I could always be Stewart the Amphibian," Kermit said once they were outside.

"Rex the Jazz Canine," Rowlf suggested.

"Leonardo D.," Gonzo declared.

"Isn't that someone already?" Fozzie asked.

"Yeah," Gonzo said, nodding. "Me."

Walter had heard enough. "This is serious!" he shouted. "You're the Muppets! No one has forgotten you!"

It sounded pretty convincing until some random passerby stepped on Gonzo.

"Well, maybe that guy has forgotten you, but that's not the point." Walter started again. "The world needs you—a world without the Muppets is a world without laughter. Without rainbows and daydreams and Swedish Chefs and boomerang fish. And that's not a world I want to live in. Now, we need to put on a show, and all we need is a little heart, a lot of determination, and a celebrity who will work for scale. Now, who's with me?"

The Muppets broke out into a cheer and Kermit gave Walter a big hug. Gary was so proud of his best friend, but there was also another feeling that he couldn't quite put his finger on. He couldn't be... jealous? While the Muppets went back to the theater to rehearse, Gary went in search of Mary. He was feeling just awful about their argument and wanted to make things right.

When he got back to the hotel, Mary wasn't there. But GARY AND MARY'S THINGS TO DO IN L.A. list was, all checked off. Mary had done everything alone. Eventually, she appeared in the doorway.

Before she could speak, Gary presented her with fresh, uncrushed daffodils. Mary smiled. How could she stay mad at him?

"What's the plan for tomorrow?" she asked sweetly. The flowers were beautiful.

"Tomorrow?" Gary asked innocently.

Just as quickly as she had melted, Mary snapped. "Okay, fine," she said, throwing the flowers down on the bed and turning back toward the door. "That's just perfect. I'm going out for a walk. By myself."

She slammed the door, leaving Gary more than a little confused. What was so important about tomorrow?

O kay, Muppets," Kermit announced the next morning. "Today we have to find a celebrity host! Otherwise, the show is canceled. Let's go!"

But hunting down a celebrity host was even harder than Kermit thought it would be. As it turned out, it was actually illegal to stage a fake awards ceremony in order to lure celebrities into a trap and bribe them to host your show. When the police showed up, Kermit's schedule got a bit off track. So things were not going well.

In the theater, Gary and Walter carried on prepping the stage for the show, but they were having some trouble concentrating. Both of the guys had big worries on their minds.

"What am I going to do?" Walter said finally. "Kermit's wrong. I don't have a talent."

"No, he's not," Gary reassured him. "You just don't know what it is yet. Hey, remember when you started break-dancing in the restaurant that time?"

Walter didn't look amused. "I was choking on a cashew nut."

"How about that motivational speech you gave the Muppets?" Gary suggested. "That was pretty amazing."

"Motivational speeches do not make a good stage act." Walter was overcome with a strange feeling. It was like he was…angry? "You're not helping!"

"Now, wait a minute," Gary replied in a tone that felt weird. "I've done nothing but help! And why is my voice getting all high and loud?"

"Why is mine getting loud to match yours?" Walter stood up.

"It's like we're in a fight!" Gary stood up, too. If he hadn't been four feet taller than his friend, it would have been kind of confrontational.

"Yeah, it's exactly like we're in a fight." Walter poked his buddy. "And if we're in a fight, you're the one who's wrong."

"Nuh-uh," Gary said, poking him back. "I've been renovating the theater and sewing costumes for a pig all day! For *you*!"

"You're just mad because"—Walter took a deep breath—"for the first time in my life, I'm somewhere I fit in!"

"What are you talking about?" By now, Gary's voice was very high and very loud. "I gave up my vacation for you! This was supposed to be the vacation where I took Mary out for our fancy dinner for our tenth anniversary and— Oh, no!" He paused to look at his watch. Only he wasn't wearing a watch. "What day is it today?" he asked.

"Friday," Walter told him.

"Oh, oh, that's bad!" Gary clapped his hand to his forehead with a big smack. "That's really bad. Oh, Mary! I've got to go! I'm an idiot!"

Without explaining to Walter, he ran out of the theater and back to the hotel. Where he arrived mysteriously wearing a tuxedo...but it was too late. The room was empty, and all of Mary's things were gone.

He had messed up the anniversary dinner.

Walter was still sitting in the theater, trying to work out just exactly what had happened, when his phone rang. He was sure it would be Gary, calling to apologize, but instead, Kermit's number flashed up on the screen.

"Hello?" Walter answered. "Oh, no! Of course, right away."

He hung up and stared at his phone for a moment before pressing the number one speed-dial button.

Back in the hotel, Gary's phone rang. He saw Walter's name flash up on the screen and ignored it for a moment. He was too sad about Mary leaving to talk to Walter. But when the phone rang a second time, he sighed. This wasn't Walter's fault; it was his own mistake. He couldn't abandon his buddy when he needed him.

"What's up, Walter?" he answered. He listened for a moment and then said, "Okay, I'll be right there."

As he stood to leave, he spotted a note on the nightstand. It was from Mary.

Gary, I love you, but you need to decide, he read to himself. *Are you a man or a Muppet? Mary xxx*

Outside the police station, Walter and Gary were having their very first official awkward moment.

"Hey," Gary said quietly. "I'm sorry about the fight."

"I'm sorry, too," Walter said.

"We'll always be best friends," Gary went on. "That will never change. It's just...I also want to be with Mary. I don't want to lose her. She's so great."

"She's the best," Walter agreed. "Far too good for you, actually."

"Really?" Gary frowned. "Are you still fighting with me?"

"No," Walter said, grinning. "I was just being cute."

"Okay, I'm sorry, I just gotta go back to Smalltown and get Mary back." Gary stuck his hands in his pockets. "I just have to."

Walter nodded. He knew what Gary had to do, but it was the worst timing. "What am I going to do without you?" he asked. "How will I figure out what to perform?"

"Listen," Gary said, kneeling down so he was eye to eye with his best bud. "I know you can do it without me. I'll always be there for you, but I think you're meant to be here, with the Muppets."

He was right. All those years that Walter had

spent feeling out of place in Smalltown were over. The few days he had spent with the Muppets had been the happiest of his life. "And you're meant to be there with Mary," he agreed. "I can see that."

Honestly, it was so sad. And to make it a little sadder, they hugged. For a really, really long time. Like, awkwardly long.

"Hey, Gary," Walter said when they finally broke apart. "Thanks for...everything."

"Sure." Gary shrugged. "No problem."

And with that, Gary headed back to Smalltown, USA, and Walter went on to his destiny, aka the police station.

Once Walter had gotten the Muppets released, everyone gathered on the sidewalk and waited for Kermit to tell them what to do. Except, he didn't. Instead, he turned and walked in the other direction.

"Sorry, guys," he said. "I thought we could win this thing, but it looks like we can't."

For a moment, they just stood and watched as Kermit walked away.

"I don't think so," a voice said. It was Piggy. "We're not going to let that bully beat the Muppets! We have to get things back on track!"

Everyone cheered.

"And we have to do it for Kermit," she added. "Now, let's get our celebrity host!"

A little while later, Animal stood on the doorstep of a nice house in the Hollywood Hills. He looked around nervously and pressed the doorbell.

"Animal!" the sponsor from the rehab center said as he opened the door. Not only was he quick to anger, he was also a super-famous, award-winning actor, which made him the perfect celebrity host. "What are you doing?"

"Acting," Animal said slowly. "Acting natural."

"NOW!" Miss Piggy screamed, and the other Muppets swooped in to grab the actor. They quickly bundled him into the car and motored over to Kermit's office.

"Kermie," Miss Piggy said as she let herself in the office, where she found the frog looking miserable. "We have our celeb, and he's a good one."

"You do?" Kermit couldn't believe it. "Where is he?"

"In the trunk," Piggy replied.

"Piggy!" He really couldn't believe it. "Kidnapping celebrities is illegal!"

"What's more illegal?" Piggy tried to reason with her frog. "Grabbing an actor or destroying the Muppets?"

"Kidnapping!" Kermit yelled. "The answer is always kidnapping."

Piggy batted her eyelashes. "But we did it for you. You inspire us."

Kermit was at a complete loss. "To what, kidnap people?"

"No," she replied. "To work together."

The other Muppets crept in the door.

"And besides, man, a celebrity is not technically a person," Janice added.

"Come on, Kermit," Miss Piggy urged. "You're the one who never gives up."

Kermit sighed. What was it that people always said? If you can't beat them . . . join them?

"Scooter," he said, standing up and crossing the room, "call a good lawyer, because after we pull off this show, we're going to have a lot of lawsuits."

"Yes, sir!" Scooter saluted and the gang ran out cheering. They had Kermit back! They were going to have a show! They were going to be in trouble with the law again . . . but after the show!

"Thanks, Piggy," Kermit said. "I . . ."

She waited. Was this it? Was this the moment he would finally say the words she needed to hear?

"Well, what are we doing here, standing around? We've got a show to put on!" he cried, and then they all marched out the door.

In Smalltown, Mary had been miserable since she arrived home alone. She missed Gary. Sure, Gary spent a lot of time with Walter, but they were best friends. It was kind of great that he had someone in his life he cared so much about. And he really was a nice guy who just wanted to help. She only wished he cared a little more about her. If he would just appear around the corner from out of nowhere with a bunch of daffodils, everything would be perfect.

"Hey, Mary," Gary said, appearing from out of nowhere, carrying a bunch of daffodils.

She jumped to her feet. It was him! It was really him!

"You're here!" She dashed down the steps and

into Gary's arms. "You came back! Where's Walter?"

"He's in L.A., where he belongs," Gary said. "And I'm where I belong. Here, with you."

At last, Mary thought as they hugged. Everything was going to be okay.

Things weren't going quite so well at the Muppet Theater. The doors had been open for hours and the only person in the audience was a hobo named Joe who wandered in off the street. And Veronica, the television exec, was glowering in the wings, accompanied by her bickering twin daughters.

"Hey, frog," she said, cornering Kermit on his way backstage, "you'd better make this work."

"Yes, Veronica." Kermit gulped. "Sure thing."

The Muppets were assembled backstage, all of them more nervous than they had ever been.

"Now, I know we don't have much of an audience out there tonight," Kermit admitted. "But that never stopped us before. We never used to care whether or not we had an audience — we performed because we loved performing."

"That's right," Scooter remembered. "We were just ourselves, and the audience came. Not the other way around."

"Who needs the audience when we've got each other?" Gonzo yelled.

"Exactly!" Kermit agreed. "Who cares if no one wants to watch us? Who cares if we're a little rusty? We're together again like a family, and that's what matters. Now, positions, everybody—let's all go break our legs!"

"Three seconds to air," Scooter informed the cast. Everyone looked nervous. What if they couldn't remember the words? What if they messed up? What if— Suddenly, the red light on the camera lit up and there was no time for what-ifs. It was time to play the music, it was time to light the lights....

Kermit leapt in front of the red velvet curtains and yelled, "It's the Muppet Telethon! YAAAAAAAY!"

Even Walter, the biggest Muppet fan ever, had to admit the opening number was a little rough — and that it was a little odd to hear Animal play the triangle instead of the drums — but at last, the show was finally happening. Kermit took to the stage once more.

"Welcome, ladies and gents, to the Muppet Telethon," he said, then paused for applause. Hobo Joe obliged. "We've got Muppets standing by to take your calls. We're here tonight because we need to raise ten million dollars to save our old studios, and we have plenty of room if you want to come down here!"

Over in Tex's office, Tex, Uncle Deadly, and the Moopets watched the show on TV.

As the camera panned around to show the empty theater, Tex relaxed in his chair. This was priceless. "Turns out America doesn't care about the Muppets after all," he said with a sneer.

"Maybe they didn't give enough notice," Uncle Deadly mused.

Tex grabbed his henchman by the neck. "You a fan or something?"

"Of course not," the dragon replied quickly. "Down with the Muppets, et cetera."

"Good," Tex said, relaxing his grip. "The end of the Muppets! Live on TV! Someone fetch me a soda. Maniacal laugh! Maniacal laugh!"

In Smalltown, USA, Gary and Mary were finally having their fancy anniversary dinner. Okay, so it was on the porch of their house, with the portable TV resting on the windowsill as they watched the Muppet Telethon, but still, it was happening and they were both happy. Or at least they were until they saw the empty theater seats on the television screen.

"There's no one there!" Gary was shocked. "It's empty!"

"Poor Walter." Mary couldn't stand to see Gary looking so distraught. "Maybe we should go back? To show support?"

Gary paused. Part of him really wanted to be there to hold Walter's hand—metaphorically and not literally, of course. Well, not unless Walter asked. But he'd made his decision, and he belonged here with Mary.

"No way," he decided. "I want to stay here with you and this amazing Cornish game hen." And with that he tucked into his dinner.

But Mary wasn't convinced.

On-screen, Gonzo was just about to start his famous bowling-ball trick. Except this time, he was doing it without the remote-control bowling ball, and with the famous celebrity actor they had "persuaded" to be on the show.

"Please don't do this," the actor begged. He stared directly into the camera. "I'm being held against my will! Why is no one helping me?"

"I'm a little stuck here.... Just a minute," Gonzo said, trying to pry his fingers out of the bowling ball.

In a living room somewhere in America, a bored mom and her daughter were watching *Credit Card Club*—a television reality show about teenagers with credit cards. The mom sighed. "Plastic-tastic"? Really? Did kids honestly talk this way? She flicked through the channels until she came to the Muppets' telethon. Gonzo was still trying to yank his hand out of the bowling ball while the actor listed his many humanitarian deeds in an effort to be rescued. The little girl laughed. Surprised by the odd noise coming from her child, the mom read the phone number on the TV screen and picked up the phone. At the theater, a phone rang. Sweetums picked up and listened to the caller on the line.

"You want to give us money?" Sweetums looked shocked and confused.

"Say yes!" yelled Kermit. This was it! The first donation!

"We gotta da money!" Sweetums shouted. And it wasn't just the donations that were starting to stream in—people were pouring through the doors, and almost every seat in the theater was full. Hobo Joe looked pleased with his new friends. At home, celebrities were calling their agents to see why they hadn't been informed about the telethon. The Muppets were officially a hit.

"You're up next, Walter," Kermit told the newbie. "Ready?"

Walter looked terrified.

"Don't sweat it," Scooter told him. "Just pretend you're naked. I mean, pretend *you're* naked, I mean, oh…Good luck!" He gave Walter a thumbs-up and left him alone behind the curtain.

"Next up, we have a talented new addition to

our show," Kermit started to announce Walter. "Meet Wal—"

Before Kermit could even finish his name, Walter started to yell and bolted off the stage, leaving a Walter-shaped hole in the wall.

"I guess we'll come back to Walter later," Kermit told the audience. "Here's Fozzie Bear!"

The Muppet comedian took the stage to a huge round of applause and pulled nervously on his bow tie. There were a lot of faces watching him, and it had been a long time since he'd performed.

"What do you call the bear capital of the world?" he asked the audience. "*Koala* Lumpur!"

No one laughed.

"I mean, *Bear*lin!" Fozzie clapped his hands together. Still nothing. "Am I on fire? Is it hot in here? I wish I could take off this fur coat.... Wocka! Wocka! Wocka!"

Before he could tell another joke, one of the most famous movie actors on Earth appeared behind him onstage. "Wow, you made it!" Fozzie joked.

"Just *bear*ly," the actor replied. "The traffic was *grizzly*. Wocka! Wocka! Wocka!"

The audience went crazy with laughter and applause.

"Wait a minute—I just did almost the same bear pun," Fozzie complained to the audience. "You'll laugh at his jokes, but not mine?"

"I'm a big star, Fozzie," the movie star explained. "They'll laugh at anything I do."

Backstage, Veronica and her kids were watching the show and laughing. Kermit even had famous actresses helping out with the catering now. The telethon was officially a success.

Which meant Tex Richman had some work to do.

"I'm going to have to deal with this myself," he growled, getting into his car. A few moments later, he was outside the Muppet Studios, next to the power cables. With an ax. And one really awful idea. He made one big chop, and suddenly all the lights in the theater went out. Across America, TV screens went dark.

"Who turned off the lights?" Kermit yelled. "Is everyone okay? Does anyone have any bright ideas?"

"Pass me the RG-fifty-nine ratchet crimper," a voice commanded. It was Mary!

"I love it when you talk shop," Gary said, handing Mary her toolbox. He shined his flashlight on the Muppets. "Oh, hey, guys."

"You guys are here!" Kermit had never been so happy to see a school shop teacher and her boyfriend in his whole life.

"We are," Gary said with a nod. "Hey, where's Walter?"

The Muppets shrugged. He hadn't been seen since he'd run off the stage. As soon as the lights came back on, Kermit announced the next musical act.

Outside, Tex Richman heard the music and couldn't believe it. The Muppets were still on the air?

"Deadly!" he shouted. "Come with me — we're going to have to shut them up once and for all."

Tex and Deadly scrambled up to the roof and perched precariously next to a giant antenna.

"To the end of the Muppets!" Tex yelled, holding a huge pair of wire cutters to the antenna. But before he could commit the awful deed, Uncle Deadly grabbed the cutters and tossed them off the roof.

"What are you doing?" Richman asked his henchman.

"Enough is enough," replied Uncle Deadly. "Just because I have a terrifying name and an evil English accent does not preclude the fact that in my heart I am a Muppet, not a Moopet. Looks like *I'm* the one who will have the last laugh!"

Tex looked shocked. "What does that mean?"

"It's a pun," Deadly explained. "Because you cannot laugh! Ha ha ha!"

And with that, he sent Tex flying off the roof. Which was still kind of an evil henchman thing to do, but at least it was a good thing for the Muppets.

Inside, it was finally time for Kermit and Piggy's duet. But Kermit wasn't onstage—he was in Piggy's empty dressing room. It was the only room in the theater he hadn't visited yet, but it was just the same as it had ever been. He opened a drawer to find half of the wedding photo Piggy had torn up in his office all those years ago—the half with just Kermit. He sighed.

"Chief?" Scooter was at the door.

"Give me a moment, Scooter," Kermit said, gently stroking the picture.

Scooter ran back to the stage and racked his brain for a filler act to go on until Kermit was ready.

"I can help," volunteered a guy dressed in a cheap superhero costume sitting in the audience. "I can make everyone's wallet disappear!" He jumped up and passed around a large, empty sack. Excited to see a magic trick, the audience members placed their wallets in the bag.

Once the bag was full, the superhero guy cackled and then ran out the door as fast as his legs could carry him. It took a while for everyone to realize they'd been robbed. Which was a little embarrassing for them.

Kermit had gone back into his own office and was looking at the Miss Piggy half of the wedding photo.

"You saved it?" Piggy asked from the doorway. "All this time?"

"Piggy?" Kermit looked up, startled.

"Oh, Kermie." She held her photo half side by side with his.

"It's always been you, Piggy, always," Kermit admitted.

"I know, Kermie," Miss Piggy said. "And you to me. Always."

It was the most romantic moment that had ever come to pass between a frog and a pig.

"I'm just not real good at saying these things, but…" He paused.

"Yes, Kermie?" Piggy needed to hear the words. Because if he didn't say them now, she was going to karate-chop him.

"Over the past few weeks, I've come to realize that *I* miss you," he said with a gulp. "And *I* need you. I know you're a performer, and I would never want to change that, but…you don't need the whole *world* to love you, just one person."

"Oh, Kermie…"

At last! After all the years of waiting, of hoping, finally the pig was going to get her frog. She leaned in, puckered up her lips, and —

"Caw! Caw!"

It was Fozzie, standing next to them making bird sounds. Piggy glared at him — the moment was ruined!

"Just trying to add some atmosphere," Fozzie said.

"We'll figure out the details later, Piggy!" Kermit said. "It's time for our song!"

Piggy and Kermit took to the stage for a beautiful rendition of "Rainbow Connection." The audience melted, and as Miss Piggy finally got her kiss, the donation graph spiked up to $9,999,999! They just needed one more dollar to save the Muppet Studios!

Everyone stared at the phones. Which one would ring first?

But none of the phones rang. Because outside the studio, Tex had crashed Kermit's car into the telephone poll, bringing down all the phone lines!

Eleven

Hidden in a dark corner backstage, Walter was looking at a photograph of him and Gary as scouts.

"I'll be with you, even when I'm not," Photo Gary said to Walter.

"I know, Photo Gary," Walter replied. "But it's not the same as having you here."

"I think Photo Gary is right about a lot of stuff," the real Gary said from behind Walter. "You should listen to him."

"Gary?!" Walter leapt up. It was really Gary!

"Hey, Walter." Gary gave his best friend a hug.

"How are you here?" Walter asked.

"Mary. She said we had to help our friend," Gary explained. "We saw the lights go out, but she fixed them. She's amazing."

"Wow! How's it all going out there?" Walter asked. He was so lucky to have friends like Gary and Mary. They really were awesome. "I can't face them all now. Not after I ran away."

"But they need you!" Gary said. "They've almost done it. They raised over nine and a half million dollars!"

"Wow." Walter let out a loud, tuneful whistle. "That's great," he said. "I wish I could help, but I have to face the facts: I don't have a talent."

But Gary was stunned. He had a brilliant idea. "I think you have one," he said. "Let's get your tux. You're on!"

Onstage, Kermit was freaking out. "Please," he begged the audience. "We just need one more dollar."

"But that guy took our wallets!" the audience yelled back. "We don't have any money!"

"I guess we're about to lose the studio," Piggy said with tears in her voice. "We tried our best, Kermie."

Kermit and Piggy held hands. Fozzie held Gonzo's hand. Gonzo hugged Camilla.

"We did. And we were really good," Kermit said with a sigh. "And maybe that's what matters. But all this? Lost forever? I thought I'd never see the day."

"Well, you did, frog," Tex shouted from the door of the auditorium. After being tossed off the roof and crashing Kermit's car, he was in a pretty bad way, but that's the least he deserved. He fell onto the stage. "Game over, Kermit. Get out of my theater. All of you."

The clock read 11:59—the Muppets still had one minute to save their studio. But even Kermit was out of ideas. Just as they were about to give up, Walter appeared in his tux and began to whistle.

It was beautiful. It truly was a wonderful talent,

and everyone turned to listen as he walked up to the stage. In the wings, Gary sobbed hysterically onto Mary.

"He's all grown up," he wailed, enough tears pouring down his face to drown everyone in the auditorium.

"Well, I guess that's worth a dollar," Statler said, yanking a one-dollar bill out of his pocket and tossing it onto the stage.

It floated down just as the clock struck midnight... and floated away again.

"We were so close!" Fozzie wailed.

And then the lights on the counter flickered for a second, and some commas and a decimal point suddenly lit up. They had raised only $99,999.99.

"Okay, that actually makes me feel better," Fozzie said, exhaling. "We were nowhere near."

The rest of the Muppets looked heartbroken. A couple were even crying. Mostly Gonzo.

"What are you waiting for?" Tex Richman was

the only happy person in the theater, but at least he was really, really happy. "You're standing on private property—my property. I'm telling you to leave, NOW."

Kermit's shoulders slumped. "He won, guys. Let's go."

To the sounds of Tex's hooting and hollering, the Muppets walked down the aisle of their theater one last time. It would have been a way more solemn occasion if Fozzie hadn't still been wearing his fart shoes.

"Wait!" Walter stopped stock-still in the middle of the aisle. "This isn't right! It can't end like this!"

"What can we do?" asked Rowlf. "Come on, man, I've got a lot of naps to catch up on."

"Listen, we have nothing to be ashamed of," Kermit said, putting his arm around his new friend. "Thanks to Walter here, we tried. And we failed. But we failed together, and that's not failing at all. This week was the best week of my life because I was with the people I love most in the world. I believe in you, and that's what's important, not a name or a building. It's each other. So let's start from the bottom and work our way up." Kermit looked around at all of the Muppets. "Let's walk out with our heads held high, as a family. Because that's what we are."

With smiles on their faces and a new sense of purpose, the Muppets threw open the doors to Tex Richman's theater, ready to head out into the world and make their fortunes all over again.

But maybe they didn't have to start from scratch. Outside were hundreds of people, chanting their name over and over and over.

"Your fans!" Walter gasped. "They came!"

"Muppets! Muppets! Muppets!" the crowd yelled. It was a crazy scene.

"Stop saying that!" Tex bellowed. "I own that!

You're breaking the law!" He turned to face the grinning Muppets. "And you can't be happy! Only people with a lot of money can be happy. That's why I'm happy!"

"You know," Gonzo said, shaking the bowling ball from his hand one more time, "I think I finally figured out how to—"

Before he finished the sentence, the ball flew off his hand and hurtled back into the theater, smacking Tex Richman square in the chops.

"*Oil* bet that hurt," Fozzie punned.

Tex stared at Fozzie for a moment. Then something snapped, and he began to laugh. It was weak and cackly at first, but then he laughed hard and loud.

"*Oil* bet that hurt!" he repeated. "I get it, because it sounds like *I'll* bet that hurt! You made me laugh! Finally!"

"Are you kidding?" Fozzie had never been so pleased. "We're a *barrel* of laughs!"

Tex stopped laughing.

"As in oil barrel?" Fozzie explained.

"Do the other one again," Tex ordered.

"*Oil* bet that hurt?" he tried.

Tex began laughing again, so hard that he could barely breathe. "You finally made me laugh! Darn it, you can have your names back."

The newly renamed Muppets cheered loudly.

"Can we have the theater back?" Fozzie asked hopefully.

"No way." Tex suddenly stopped laughing. "There's oil under there."

"Hey, Richman!" Miss Poogy and the rest of the Moopets appeared, looking less than impressed. "We had a deal!"

"In your face, Moopets," Uncle Deadly cackled as Tex began laughing again. It was one of those once you start, you just can't stop kind of things, and Tex had a lifetime of laughter to catch up on.

Kermit took Piggy's arm and smiled. At last,

everything was great. Piggy was back by his side, the Muppets were back together, Walter had found where he belonged, and, well, there was only one thing left to do. Kermit nodded at his new friend Gary, and Piggy giggled.

Gary turned to Mary—she really was amazing. He bent down on one knee and pulled out a ring. Mary gasped.

"I just have one question for you," he said, holding out a ring. "Will you, Mary, marry me?"

Mary looked at Gary, looked at the Muppets, looked at Walter, and then, with love in her eyes, she turned to face the audience, opened her mouth, and said the only thing she could possibly say: "Mahna mahna! Mahna mahna!"

(Okay, so she sang a song with the Muppets, and then she said "YES!")

THE END